One Grain of Rice

A MATHEMATICAL FOLKTALE

Demi

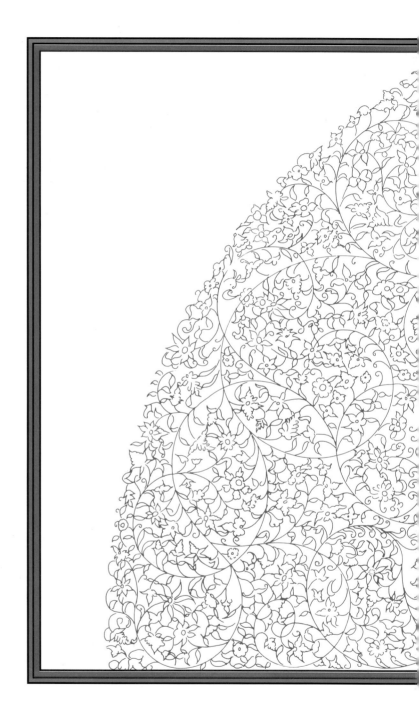

SCHOLASTIC INC.

New York Toronto London Auckland Sydney

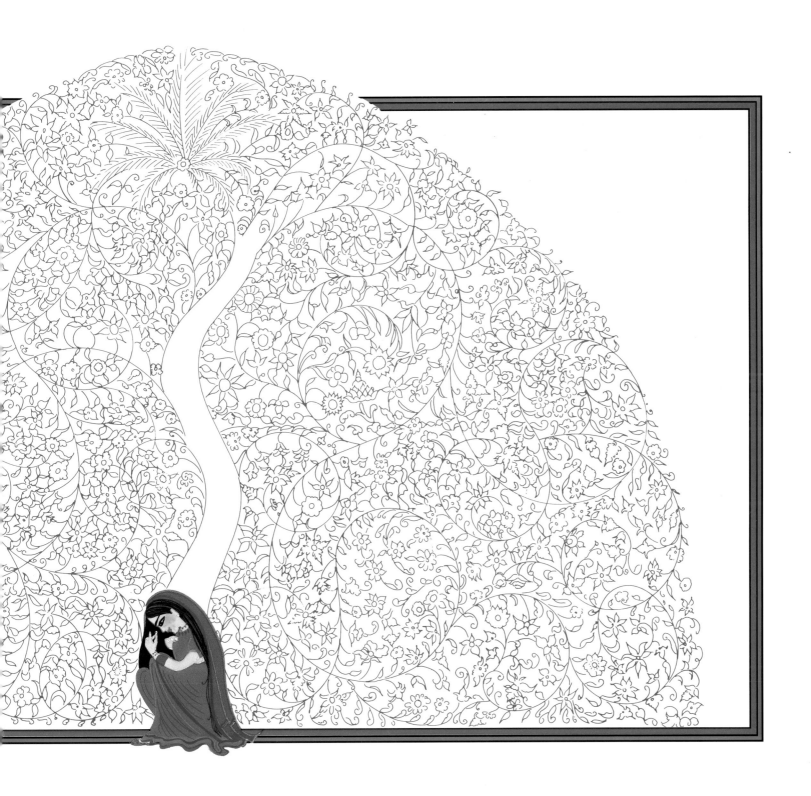

For JAN STEWARD,
who gave to me her love of India

And 1,073,741,823 thanks to my magical editor, Lauren Thompson

ISBN 0-590-93999-8

12 11 10 9 8 7 6 5   10   8 9/9 0 1 2/0

Printed in the U.S.A.   08

Book design by Marijka Kostiw
Text type set in 14 pt. Cochin
Handlettering by Anton Kimball

For the illustrations in this book, Demi was inspired by traditional Indian miniature paintings of the sixteenth and seventeenth centuries. She created the artwork using Chinese brushes and a variety of paints and inks.

A traditional version of this Indian tale is recorded as "Sissa and the Troublesome Trifles" in *Trickster Tales* by I.G. Edmonds.

Long ago in India, there lived a raja who believed that he was wise and fair, as a raja should be.

The people in his province were rice farmers. The raja decreed that everyone must give nearly all of their rice to him.

"I will store the rice safely," the raja promised the people, "so that in time of famine, everyone will have rice to eat, and no one will go hungry."

Each year, the raja's rice collectors gathered nearly all of the people's rice and carried it away to the royal storehouses.

For many years, the rice grew well. The people gave nearly all of their rice to the raja, and the store-houses were always full. But the people were left with only just enough rice to get by.

Then one year the rice grew badly,
and there was famine and hunger.
The people had no rice to give
to the raja, and they had no rice
to eat.

The raja's ministers implored him, "Your Highness, let us open the royal storehouses and give the rice to the people, as you promised."

"No!" cried the raja. "How do I know how long the famine may last? I must have the rice for myself. Promise or no promise, a raja must not go hungry!"

Time went on, and the people
grew more and more hungry.
But the raja would not give out
the rice.

One day, the raja ordered a feast for himself and his court — as, it seemed to him, a raja should now and then, even when there is famine.

A servant led an elephant from a royal storehouse to the palace, carrying two full baskets of rice.

A village girl named Rani saw that a trickle of rice was falling from one of the baskets. Quickly she jumped up and walked along beside the elephant, catching the falling rice in her skirt. She was clever, and she began to make a plan.

At the palace, a guard cried, "Halt, thief! Where are you going with that rice?"

"I am not a thief," Rani replied. "This rice fell from one of the baskets, and I am returning it now to the raja."

When the raja heard about Rani's good deed, he asked his ministers to bring her before him.

"I wish to reward you for returning what belongs to me," the raja said to Rani. "Ask me for anything, and you shall have it."

"Your Highness," said Rani, "I do not deserve any reward at all. But if you wish, you may give me one grain of rice."

"Only one grain of rice?" exclaimed the raja. "Surely you will allow me to reward you more plentifully, as a raja should."

"Very well," said Rani. "If it pleases Your Highness, you may reward me in this way. Today, you will give me a single grain of rice. Then, each day for thirty days you will give me double the rice you gave me the day before. Thus, tomorrow you will give me two grains of rice, the next day four grains of rice, and so on for thirty days."

"This seems still to be a modest reward," said the raja. "But you shall have it."

And Rani was presented with a single grain of rice.

The next day, Rani was presented with two grains of rice.

And the following day, Rani was presented with four grains of rice.

On the ninth day, Rani was presented with two hundred and fifty-six grains of rice. She had received in all five hundred and eleven grains of rice, only enough for a small handful.

"This girl is honest, but not very clever," thought the raja. "She would have gained more rice by keeping what fell into her skirt!"

On the twelfth day, Rani received two thousand and forty-eight grains of rice, about four handfuls. On the thirteenth day, she received four thousand and ninety-six grains of rice, enough to fill a bowl.

On the sixteenth day, Rani was presented with a bag containing thirty-two thousand, seven hundred and sixty-eight grains of rice. All together she had enough rice for two full bags.

"This doubling adds up to more rice than I expected!" thought the raja. "But surely her reward won't amount to much more."

On the twentieth day, Rani was presented with sixteen more bags filled with rice.

On the twenty-first day, she received one million, forty-eight thousand, five hundred and seventy-six grains of rice, enough to fill a basket.

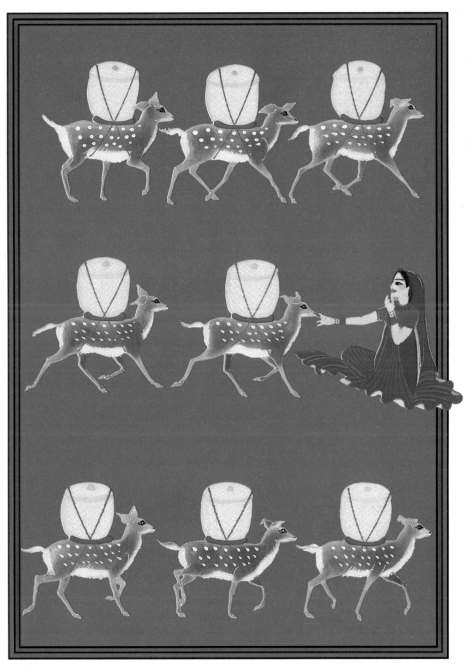

On the twenty-fourth day, Rani was presented with eight million, three hundred and eighty-eight thousand, six hundred and eight grains of rice — enough to fill eight baskets, which were carried to her by eight royal deer.

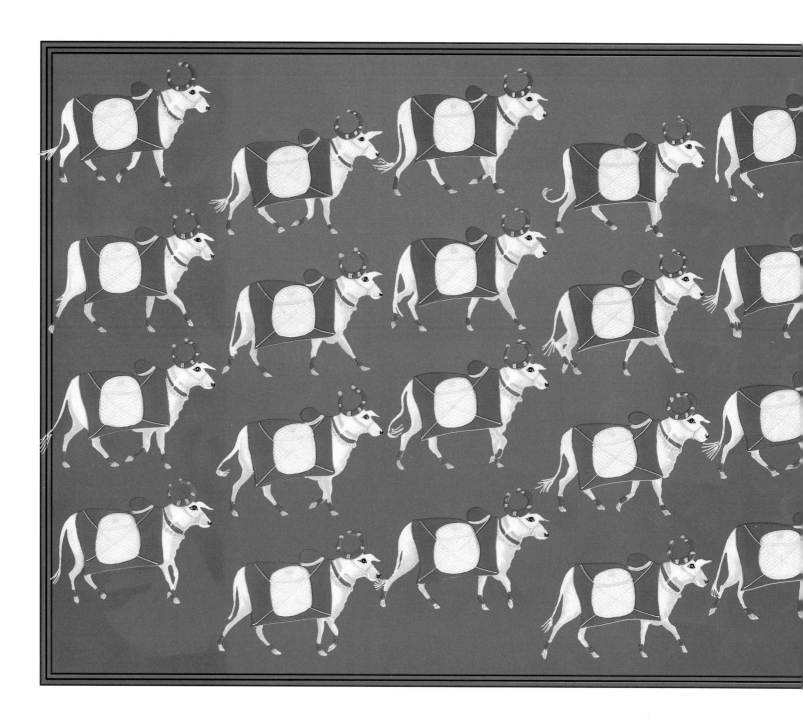

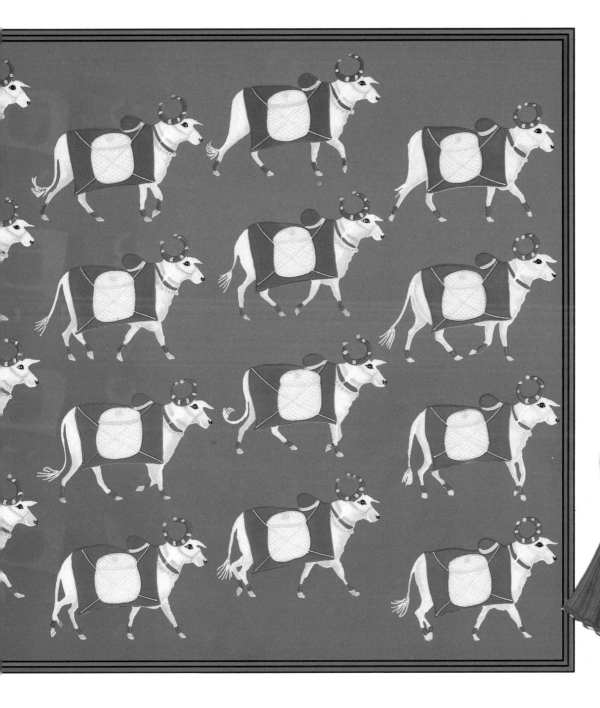

On the twenty-seventh day, thirty-two Brahma bulls were needed to deliver sixty-four baskets of rice.

The raja was deeply troubled. "One grain of rice has grown very great indeed," he thought. "But I shall fulfill the reward to the end, as a raja should."

On the twenty-ninth day, Rani
was presented with the contents of
two royal storehouses.

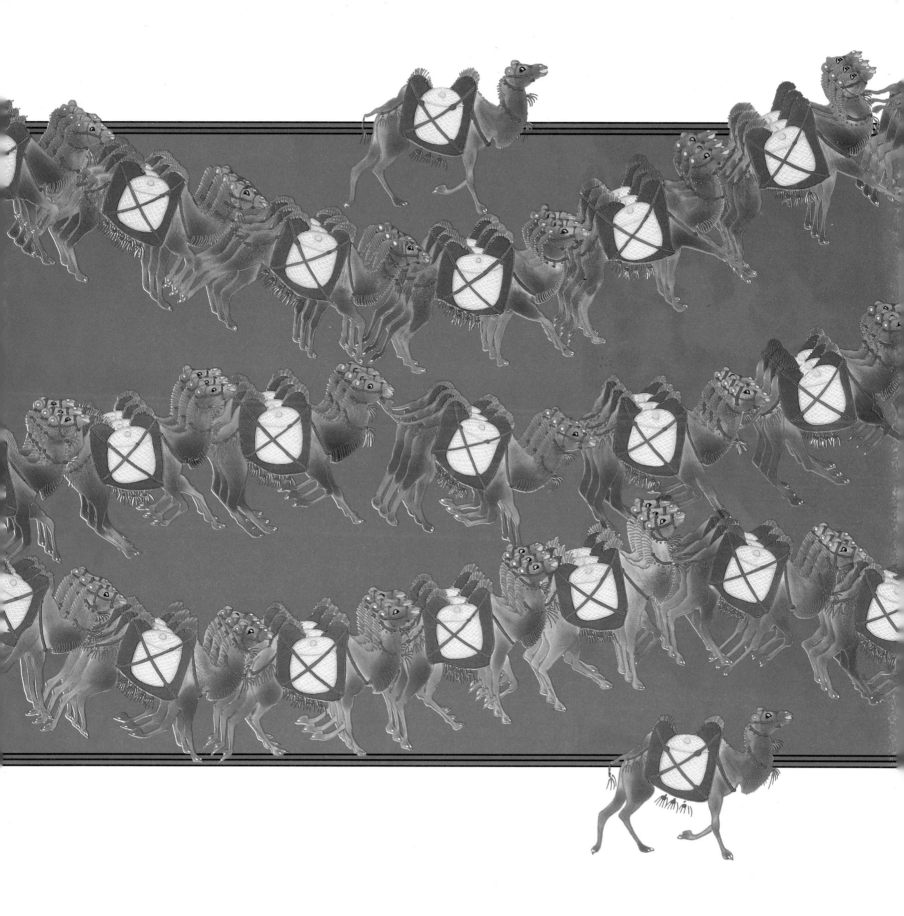

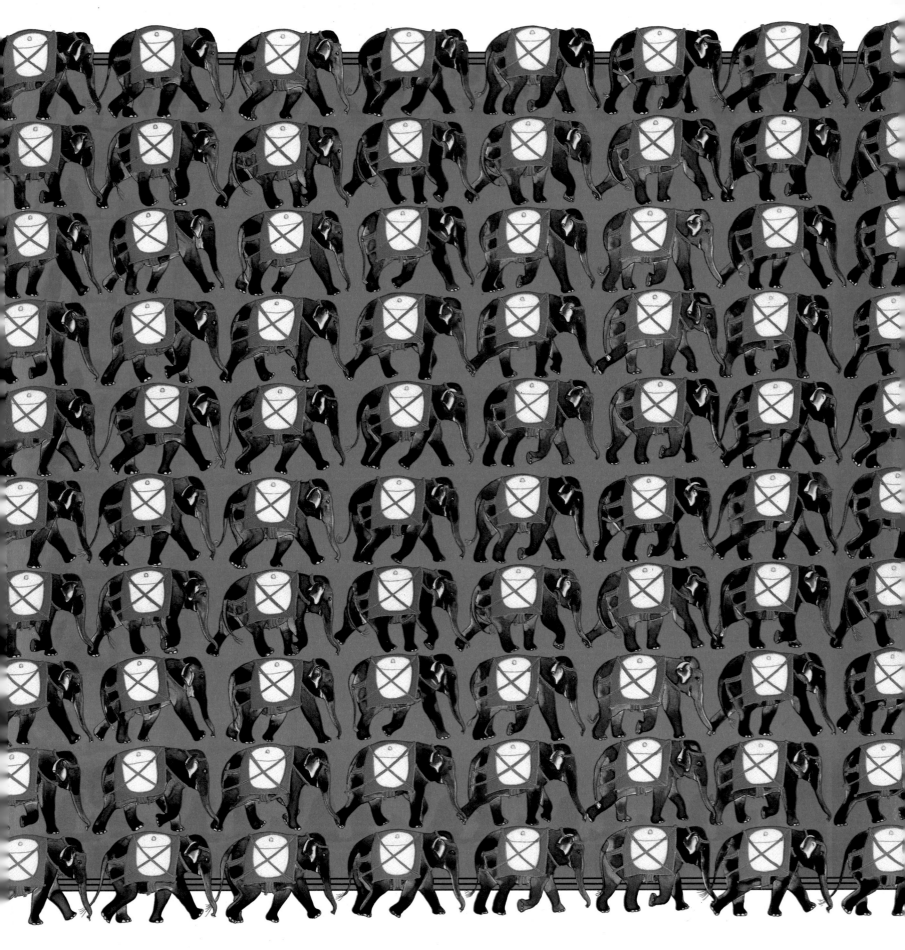

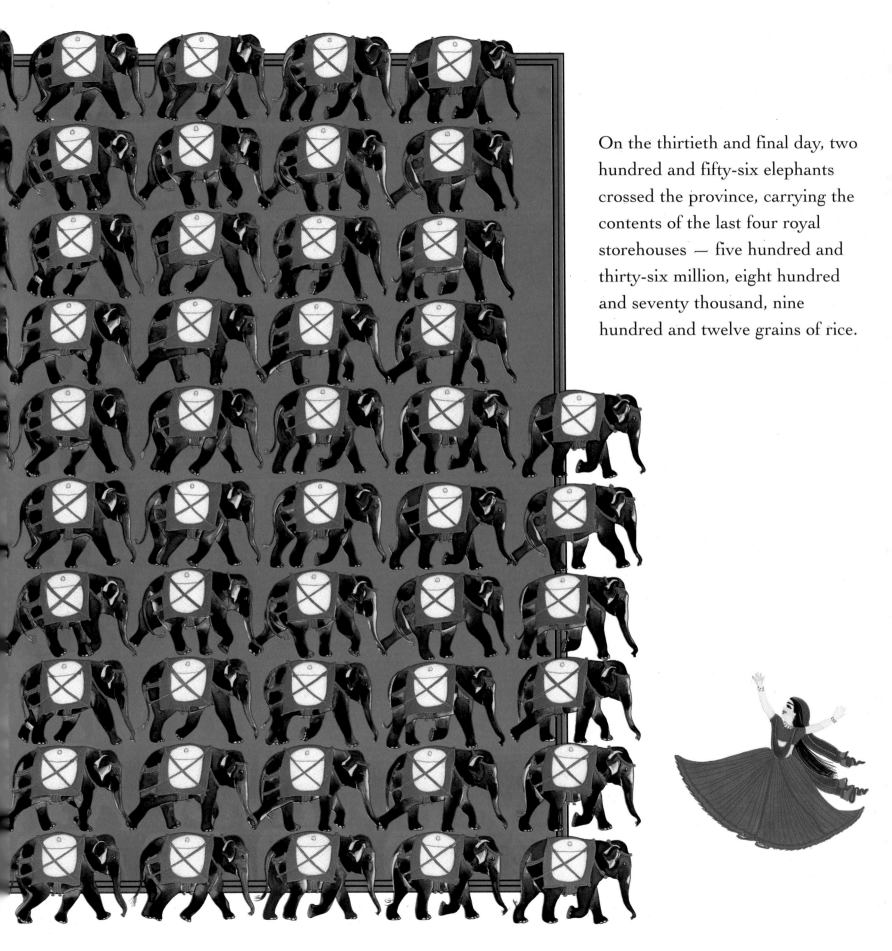

On the thirtieth and final day, two hundred and fifty-six elephants crossed the province, carrying the contents of the last four royal storehouses — five hundred and thirty-six million, eight hundred and seventy thousand, nine hundred and twelve grains of rice.

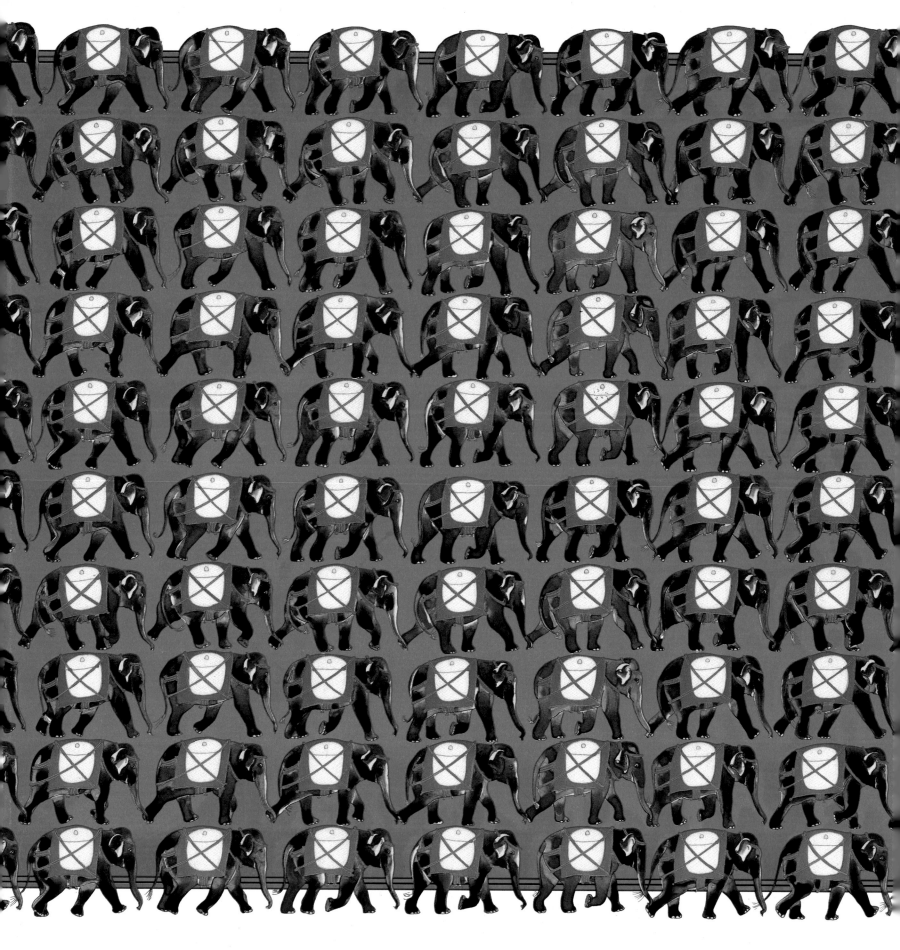

All together, Rani had received more than one billion grains of rice. The raja had no more rice to give. "And what will you do with this rice," said the raja with a sigh, "now that I have none?"

"I shall give it to all the hungry people," said Rani. "And I shall leave a basket of rice for you, too, if you promise from now on to take only as much rice as you need."

"I promise," said the raja.

And for the rest of his days, the raja was truly wise and fair, as a raja should be.

FROM ONE GRAIN OF RICE TO ONE BILLION

Each day, Rani received double the amount of rice as the day before.
See how quickly one grain of rice doubles into so much more.

Day 1	Day 2	Day 3	Day 4	Day 5
1 *grain of rice*	**2** *grains of rice*	**4** *grains of rice*	**8** *grains of rice*	**16** *grains of rice*
Day 6	Day 7	Day 8	Day 9	Day 10
32 *grains of rice*	**64** *grains of rice*	**128** *grains of rice*	**256** *grains of rice*	**512** *grains of rice*
Day 11	Day 12	Day 13	Day 14	Day 15
1,024 *grains of rice*	**2,048** *grains of rice*	**4,096** *grains of rice*	**8,192** *grains of rice*	**16,384** *grains of rice*
Day 16	Day 17	Day 18	Day 19	Day 20
32,768 *grains of rice*	**65,536** *grains of rice*	**131,072** *grains of rice*	**262,144** *grains of rice*	**524,288** *grains of rice*
Day 21	Day 22	Day 23	Day 24	Day 25
1,048,576 *grains of rice*	**2,097,152** *grains of rice*	**4,194,304** *grains of rice*	**8,388,608** *grains of rice*	**16,777,216** *grains of rice*
Day 26	Day 27	Day 28	Day 29	Day 30
33,554,432 *grains of rice*	**67,108,864** *grains of rice*	**134,217,728** *grains of rice*	**268,435,456** *grains of rice*	**536,870,912** *grains of rice*

To count how many grains of rice Rani received in all, add all of these numbers together.
The answer: 1,073,741,823 — more than one billion grains of rice!